Patch

Patch

by Kristin Earhart
illustrated by Lisa Papp

SCHOLASTIC INC.

New York   Toronto   London   Auckland   Sydney
Mexico City   New Delhi   Hong Kong   Buenos Aires

To all my friends at Riverlea
- K. J. E.

For Kelly and Jemel
- L. P.

Library of Congress Cataloging-in-Publication Data

Earhart, Kristin.
Patch / by Kristin Earhart ; illustrated by Lisa Papp.
p. cm. -- (Breyer stablemates)
"Cartwheel books."
Summary: Lauren is friendly with Sarah even after the new girl brags that her horse is much better than Lauren's,
but when Sarah gets in trouble while riding in the woods, Lauren and her horse come to the rescue.
ISBN 0-439-72236-5 (hardcover)
[1. Friendship--Fiction. 2. Behavior--Fiction. 3. Horses--Fiction.] I. Papp, Lisa, ill. II. Title. III. Series.
PZ7.E124New 2006
[E]--dc22   2005008424

12 11 10 9 8 7 6 5 4 3 2 1   6 7 8 9 10

Printed in China   62
First printing, March 2006

Table of Contents

At Tall Trees Stable

Many horses lived at Tall Trees Stable. One horse was black and white. Her name was Patch. Patch belonged to Lauren.

Lauren loved Patch. Patch used to win ribbons in horse shows. But she was older now.

Patch didn't like to jump anymore. So Lauren and Patch liked to ride in the woods together.

One day, Lauren saw a new girl at the stable.

"Hi, I'm Lauren," she said. "This is my horse, Patch."

"I'm Sarah," the new girl said. "This is my horse, Gold Charm."

Patch whinnied a friendly hello to Gold Charm.

"Gold Charm jumps fences," said Sarah.
"We win lots of ribbons. Gold Charm is
the best horse. She is better than Patch."
Then Sarah led Gold Charm away.

Gold Charm was beautiful. She had a golden coat. Her mane and tail were long and white.

Lauren went into Patch's stall.

"You don't have to win ribbons
anymore," she told her horse. "I love you
anyway."

In the Ring

Lauren put a saddle and bridle on Patch. She led Patch outside. Sarah was riding Gold Charm around the ring. Lauren and Patch watched.

Sarah stopped Gold Charm.

"We are going to jump now," she said.

Sarah and Gold Charm jumped all of the fences.

"I bet Gold Charm can jump better than Patch," Sarah said.

Lauren knew that Patch was a good jumper. But she did not want to show off for Sarah.

"I am not jumping Patch today,"
Lauren said. "We are going for a ride in
the woods."

"I want to go in the woods, too,"
Sarah said. "We'll come with you." Gold
Charm trotted out of the ring.

Sarah and Gold Charm passed Lauren
and Patch.

"We will go first," Sarah called.

Into the Woods

Patch followed Gold Charm into the woods. The trees were tall. The woods were dark. The wind blew. And the trees seemed to be moving!

Lauren and Patch could tell that Gold Charm did not like the woods. She took high steps. She was scared. She snorted and stopped.

Sarah wanted Gold Charm to keep walking. But Gold Charm wouldn't move. Just then, a big black-and-white bird flew down. The bird flapped its wings. It flew by Gold Charm's head. She jumped forward and started to run!

Gold Charm galloped through the
trees. She jumped over a fence. Sarah
held on tight. But she could not stop
Gold Charm.

Lauren and Patch raced after Gold
Charm. They galloped through the trees.
They jumped over the same fence that
Gold Charm had jumped over.

They caught up with Sarah and Gold
Charm. Patch whinnied to Gold Charm.
Gold Charm slowed down.

"Are you okay?" Lauren asked.

"Yes," Sarah said.

"We should go back," Lauren said.
This time, Sarah and Gold Charm
followed Lauren and Patch on the trail
back to the stable.

Safe at Home

Soon they were back at the stable. The girls took off the saddles and bridles. They all went outside.

"Gold Charm was very scared in the woods," Sarah said.

"Patch was scared once, too," Lauren
said. "But we ride in the woods all the
time now."

"But Patch was so brave today,"
Sarah said. "She helped Gold Charm feel
safe. I'm sorry I said that Gold Charm is
better than Patch. Patch is a good horse."

Lauren smiled. She knew that Patch
was a good horse all along.

"Gold Charm is a good horse, too,"
she said.

Gold Charm and Patch grazed on the grass together like old friends.

"I think they're friends," Lauren said.

"Can we be friends, too?" Sarah asked.

"That would be fun," Lauren said.

The new friends smiled at each other. And they smiled at their horses.

About the Horses

Facts on Palominos:

1. Palomino horses have a gold coat and a white mane and tail.
2. The palomino is a color type and not a breed because it is found in many horse and pony breeds.
3. Palominos came to America from Spain in the 16th century.
4. Palominos are very popular parade horses.

Facts on Pintos:

1. Pintos are named for their two-color coats.
2. Pinto coats have two kinds of color patterns: one is white with large patches of color (Tobiano), and one is a darker color with patches of white (Overo).
3. The pinto is also only a color type, not a breed.
4. The Sioux and Crow Indians prized pintos for their unique coloring.

When Horses Are All You Dream About...

It has to be Breyer® model horses!

Breyer® model horses are fun to play with and collect!
Meet horse heroes that you know and love. Learn about horses
from foreign lands. Enjoy crafts and games.
Visit us at **www.BreyerHorses.com/kidsbooks**
for horse fun that never ends!